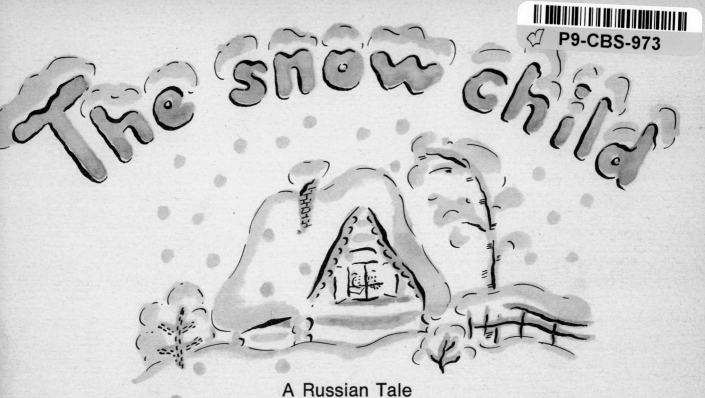

The snow child

A Russian Tale

• Retold by Freya Littledale • Illustrated by Leon Shtainmets •

SCHOLASTIC BOOK SERVICES

NEW YORK · TORONTO · LONDON · AUCKLAND · SYDNEY · TOKYO

ISBN: 0-590-05398-1

Text copyright © 1978 by Freya Littledale. Illustrations copyright © 1978 by Leon Shtainmets. All rights reserved. Published by Scholastic Book Services, a division of Scholastic Magazines, Inc.

12 11 10 9 8 7 6 5 4 3 2   9/7 0 1 2 3/8

for Marc

Once upon a time, in a far-away village,
there lived an old man and his wife.
They loved one another dearly,
but they were unhappy
because they had no children.

One cold winter day
when the first snow lay deep on the ground,
the old couple stood at the window.
The children of the village were playing outside.

They were building a snowman as big as a giant.

When the snowman was finished
and the children had gone,
the old man turned to his wife.
"Why don't we go outside
and build a snow child?" he said.

"Why not!" said his wife.
"We can make a little girl!"

So they went out to the garden
and set to work.

Slowly and carefully they shaped the snow.
They made a little body
with dainty hands and feet.
They rolled a ball of snow
and shaped the head.
Then they carved the mouth and eyes
with a tiny twig.
The snow child was as perfect as she could be.
Her dress was trimmed with icicles,
and her hair was made of willow branches
covered with frost.

"The snow child is so beautiful!" said the old man.

"How I wish she were real!" sighed his wife.
And she bent down
and kissed the child's lips.

No sooner had she done this
than the snow child came to life!
Her lips turned pink.
Warm breath came from her mouth.
And she looked at the old couple
with the eyes of a real child.

First she moved her head...
then her arms...
then her legs....

"Look!" cried the old man.
"She's alive!"

The snow child smiled,
and then she spoke:
"I am a child of the snow.
I come to you as cold winds blow."

"Our wish has come true!" said the old woman.

"Yes," said her husband,
"at last we have a little girl of our own."
And he took the snow child in his arms
and carried her into the cottage.

The old couple had never been so happy.

The old man told stories.
The old woman sang songs,
and the snow child danced
around the room.

That night the old woman made up a little bed
with a warm woolen blanket.

"Come," she said,
"it is time to go to sleep."

But the snow child shook her head.
"I cannot sleep here," she said.
"I must always sleep outside."

"You will be too cold,"
said the old woman.

"Oh no!" the snow child laughed.
"I can never be too cold!"
And out she ran
into the garden.

Every night she slept there
on a bed of snow.

And every night the old couple
looked out of the window
to make sure
their little girl was safe.

The moon and stars
shone down upon her.
And they could see
that she smiled as she slept.
All was well.

All winter long,
the snow child played with the village children.

She showed them how to make many things out of snow —
horses, a carriage, and a beautiful palace.

At last spring came,
and the sun warmed the land.
Birds returned from far-off places,
and buds opened
in the garden.

The children of the village were glad.
They danced and they sang
in the sunlight.
They called to the snow child,
"Come! Come and play with us!"

But the snow child would not go.
She hid from the sun
and sat in the shade of a willow tree
or in a dark corner of the cottage.

"What is wrong?" asked the old woman.

"Are you ill?" asked the old man.

"Nothing is wrong," she answered.
"I am fine."

Yet the snow child grew sadder and sadder
as the days grew warmer.
Her lips lost their color,
and she seemed thin and weak.

Then one morning,
when the last of the snow had melted,
she came to the old couple
and kissed them both.
"I must leave you now," she said.

"Why?" they cried.

"I am a child of the snow.
I must go where it is cold."

"No! No!" they cried.
"You cannot go!"

They held her close,
and a few drops of snow
fell to the floor.

Quickly she slipped from their arms
and ran out the door.

"Come back!" they called.
"Come back to us!"

But the snow child was gone.
And the old couple wept.
They thought
they would never see her again.

All summer long
children played,
birds sang,
and flowers bloomed
around the cottage.
But the old man and his wife
could think only
of their little girl.

Then the following winter,
when the first snow fell,
the old couple
looked out of the window.
There in the garden
stood the snow child.

They rushed outside
and kissed her.
The snow child smiled,
and then she spoke:
"I am a child of the snow.
I come back to you
as cold winds blow."

The snow child stayed with the old man and his wife
all through the winter.
Then, when spring came,
she left once more.

But the old man and his wife were no longer sad.
They knew that their snow child
would return to them
every winter forever after.